The
Jan Pieńkowski
Fairy Tale Library

Snow White
The Sleeping Beauty
Puss-in-Boots
Cinderella

Snow White

from the Brothers Grimm
with pictures by Jan Pieńkowski

Alfred A. Knopf : New York

for Sophie

This is a Borzoi Book
published by Alfred A. Knopf, Inc.

Illustrations and lettering copyright © 1977 Jan Pieńkowski
Text copyright © 1977 David Walser

ISBN: 0-679-82270-4 (Slipcase)

First Alfred A. Knopf Edition, 1992.

Manufactured in Singapore
10 9 8 7 6 5 4 3 2 1

Snow White

I t was deep mid-winter, and snowflakes were falling like feathers from the sky. A queen sat sewing at her window, which had a fine black ebony frame. As she gazed out at the white landscape, she pricked her finger with the needle and three drops of blood fell on the snow.

"If only I had a child as white as snow, as red as blood and as black as ebony," she thought.

Not long after, her wish was granted, for a daughter was born to her. The child's skin was as white as snow, her lips and cheeks as red as blood and her hair as black as ebony, so she was called Snow White. But as she was born, the queen died.

After a year, the king married again. His new wife was a beautiful woman, though so proud and overbearing that she could not endure any rival to her beauty.

She had a magic mirror and when she stood before it gazing at her own reflection she would ask:

"Mirror, mirror on the wall,
Who is the fairest one of all?"

It always replied:

"You, my Lady Queen, are the fairest one of all."

Then she was happy, for she
knew the mirror always spoke
the truth.

But Snow White was
growing prettier and
prettier every day, and
when she was seven
years old she was as beautiful as
a bright day and fairer even than
the queen herself. One day, when
the queen asked her mirror the
question, it replied:

"Though you, my Queen,
            are fair, 'tis true
Snow White is fairer far than you."

Then the queen flew into a dreadful rage and turned green and yellow with jealousy. From this hour forth, she hated the girl, and envy and malice grew like weeds in her heart so that she had no more peace day or night. One day she called a huntsman to her and said:

"Take the child out into the forest; I never want to see her face again. You must kill her and bring me back her lungs and liver as a proof she is dead."

The huntsman did as he was told and led Snow White into the forest, but as he was drawing his hunting knife to slay her, she cried out:

"Good huntsman, spare my life and I will run into the wild forest and never go home again."

She looked so pretty that the huntsman had pity on her, and said: "Well, run away, you poor child." But he thought to himself: "The wild beasts will soon eat her up," and his heart felt lighter, because he hadn't had to kill her himself. As he turned away, a young boar came running past, so he shot it and brought its lungs and liver home to the queen as a proof that Snow White was really dead. The cook was told to stew them in salt and the wicked woman ate them up, thinking she had eaten Snow White's lungs and liver.

ow the poor child found herself alone in the forest, and she felt so frightened she didn't know which way to turn. Then she began to run over the sharp stones and through bramble bushes; the wild beasts ran close by her, but

they did her no harm. Snow White ran as far as her legs would carry her and, as evening approached, she saw a little house and went inside to rest.

Everything was very small in the little house, but cleaner and neater than anything you can imagine. In the middle of the room, there stood a little table with a white tablecloth and seven little plates, each with its fork, spoon, knife and cup. Side by side against the wall, there were seven little beds, covered with shining white counterpanes.

Snow White felt so hungry and thirsty that she ate a bit of bread

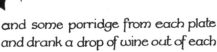

and some porridge from each plate
and drank a drop of wine out of each
cup, for she didn't want to leave anyone
without food or drink. Then, feeling
tired, she lay down on one of the beds,
but it wasn't comfortable; so she
tried all the others in turn, but one
was too long and another too short,
until she tried the seventh which was
just right. So she lay down upon it,
said her prayers and fell asleep.

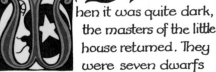

hen it was quite dark,
the masters of the little
house returned. They
were seven dwarfs
who worked up in the mountains,

digging for precious ore. They lit
their seven little lamps and saw
that someone had been there, for
the room was not so spick and span
as they had left it.

The first said:

"Who's been sitting on my chair?"

The second said:

"Who's been eating out of my plate?"

The third said:

"Who's been eating my bread?"

The fourth said:
"Who's been tasting my porridge?"
The fifth said:
"Who's been using my fork?"
The sixth said:
"Who's been cutting with my knife?"
The seventh said:
"Who's been drinking out of my cup?"
Then the first dwarf looked round
and saw a hollow in his bed so he
asked again:

"Who's been lying on my bed?"

The others came running up and each one exclaimed as he saw his bed:

"Somebody has been lying on mine too."

But when the seventh came to his bed, he saw Snow White lying there fast asleep. Then he called the others, who ran up and shone their lamps on the bed.

"Goodness gracious! Goodness gracious!" they cried, when they saw Snow White lying there. "What a beautiful child!"

They were so enchanted by her beauty that they did not wake her but let her sleep on. The seventh dwarf slept with his companions, one hour in each bed, and in this way

he managed to pass the night.

Next morning, when Snow White awoke, she saw the seven dwarfs and felt very frightened; but they were friendly and asked her what she was called.

"I am Snow White," she replied.

"How is it you came to our house?" asked the dwarfs. Then she told them how her stepmother had tried to have her put to death and how the huntsman had spared her and how she had run the whole day until she had found their house. Then the dwarfs said to her:

"If you will keep house for us, cook, make the beds, do the washing,

sewing and knitting, and keep
everything neat and clean, you can
stay with us and you shall want
for nothing."

"Yes," answered Snow White, "I
will gladly do all you ask."

nd so she made her
home with them.
Every morning the
dwarfs went into the
mountain to dig for precious ore
and gold, and in the evening when
they returned home their supper
had to be ready. But since, during
the day, the girl was left quite
alone, the good dwarfs warned her:
"Beware of your stepmother. She
will soon find out you are here, so
whatever you do, let no one into

the house."

Now the queen, after she thought
she had eaten Snow White's lungs
and liver, never doubted that she
was once more the most beautiful
woman in the world; so stepping
before her mirror one day she said:

"Mirror, mirror on the wall,
Who is the fairest one of all?"

and the mirror replied:

"Though you, my Queen,
                        are fair, 'tis true,
Snow White is fairer far than you.

O'er seventh stream and
                        seventh hill
    With seven dwarfs, she's living still."
When the queen heard these words,
her blood boiled with anger, for the
mirror always spoke the truth. She
knew now that the huntsman had
deceived her and that Snow White
was still alive. Day and night she
pondered how she might destroy her,
for as long as she felt she was not
the fairest in the land, jealousy left
her no rest. At last she hit upon a
plan. She stained her face and dressed
herself up as an old pedlar woman.
In this disguise, she set off over the
seven hills till she came to the house

of the seven
dwarfs. She
knocked at the
door, calling out:
"Fine wares for
sale, fine wares
for sale!"

Snow White
peeped out of
the window and
called to her:

"Good day, good
woman, what
have you to sell?"

"Good wares,
fine wares,"
she answered:

"laces of rainbow hues," and she held one up that was made of some bright silk.

"Surely I can let the honest woman in," thought Snow White; so she unbarred the door and bought the pretty lace.

"Good gracious! child," said the old woman, "what a mess you look! Come! I'll lace you up properly for once."

Snow White, suspecting no evil, stood before her and let her lace her bodice up, but the old woman laced her so quickly and so tightly that it took Snow White's breath away and she fell down dead.

"Now you are no longer the fairest,"

said the wicked old woman as she hastened away.

In the evening, the seven dwarfs came home. You can imagine what a fright they got when they saw their dear Snow White lying on the floor, as still and motionless as a dead person.

They lifted her up tenderly, and when they saw how tightly laced she was they cut the lace in two.

She began to breathe and little by little came back to life. When the dwarfs heard what had happened, they said:

"Why, the old pedlar woman was none other than the queen. In future you must be sure to let no one in, if we are not at home."

As soon as the wicked queen got home, she went straight to her mirror, and said:

"Mirror, mirror on the wall
Who is the fairest one of all?"
and the mirror answered as before:

"Though you, my Queen,
are fair, 'tis true,
Snow White is fairer far than you.

O'er seventh stream and seventh hill,
With seven dwarfs, she's living still."
When she heard this she was so angry the blood drained from her face, because she saw at once that Snow White must be alive again. "This time," she said to herself, "I will think of something that will make an end of you once and for all."

By means of witchcraft, which she understood well, she made a poisoned comb. Then she dressed herself up to look like another old woman and set out across the

seven hills to the house of the seven
dwarfs. Knocking at the door, she
called out: "Fine wares for sale!"

Snow White looked out of the
window and said:

"Go on your way! I am not allowed
to let anyone in."

"But surely you are not forbidden
to look?" asked the old woman, as
she pulled out the poisoned comb
and held it up for her to see.

It pleased the girl so much that
she opened the door. When they
had settled their bargain, the old

woman said:

"Now just for once, I'll comb your hair properly for you."

Poor Snow White suspected nothing, but as soon as the comb touched her hair, the poison worked and she fell down unconscious.

"Now, my fine lady, you're really

finished this time," said the wicked woman, and she made her way home as fast as she could.

Fortunately it was near evening, and the seven dwarfs returned home. When they saw Snow White lying as if dead on the ground, they at once suspected that her wicked stepmother had been at work again; so they searched till they found the poisoned comb.

The moment they pulled it out of her hair, Snow White came to herself again and told them what had happened. Then once more they warned her to be on her guard and to open the door to no one.

As soon as the queen got home,
she went straight to her mirror
and asked:

"Mirror, mirror on the wall,
Who is the fairest one of all?"

and it replied as before:

"Though you, my Queen,
          are fair, 'tis true,
Snow White is fairer far than you.
O'er seventh stream
          and seventh hill,
With seven dwarfs, she's living still."

When she heard these words she
trembled and shook with rage.
"Snow White shall die," she cried.
"Yes, even though it cost me my
own life."

hen she went to a little secret chamber, which no one knew of but herself, and there she made a poisoned apple. It looked beautiful, white and red cheeked, so that anyone who saw it longed to eat it, but anyone who did so would certainly die on the spot. When the apple was ready, she stained her face, dressed herself up as a peasant woman and set off again to the house of the seven dwarfs. She knocked at the door but Snow White put her head out of the window and called out:

"I must not let anyone in, the seven dwarfs told me not to."

"Quite right," answered the old peasant woman. "But I'll soon have no more apples. Here, I'll give you one."

"No," said Snow White, "I may not take it."

"Are you afraid of being poisoned?" asked the old woman. "See, I will cut this apple in half. I'll eat the white cheek and you can eat the red."

But the apple was so cunningly made that only the red cheek was poisoned. Snow White longed to eat the tempting fruit and when she saw that the peasant woman was eating it herself, she could resist no longer. Stretching out her hand, she took the poisoned half, but hardly had the first bite passed her lips than she fell down dead on the ground. Then the eyes of the cruel queen sparkled with pleasure, and laughing aloud she cried:

"As white as snow, as red as blood and as black as ebony! This time, the dwarfs won't be able to bring you back to life." And when she got home, she asked the mirror:

"Mirror, mirror on the wall,
    Who is the fairest one of all?"
At last it replied:

"You, my Lady Queen, are the

fairest one of all."

Then her jealous heart was at rest—
at least, as much at rest as a jealous
heart can ever be.

When the dwarfs came home
in the evening, they found Snow
White lying on the ground, and
she neither breathed nor stirred.
They lifted her up and looked every-
where to see if they could find anything
poisonous about. They unlaced her
bodice, combed her hair, washed her
with water and wine, but all in vain; the
child was dead and remained dead.

Then they placed her on a bier and
all the seven dwarfs sat round it,
weeping and sobbing for three whole

days. At last they made up their minds to bury her, but she looked so like a living being and her cheeks were still so red, that they said: "We can't hide her away in the black ground."

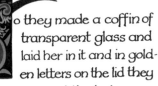

So they made a coffin of transparent glass and laid her in it and in golden letters on the lid they wrote her name and that she was a royal princess. Then they put the coffin on the top of the mountain and one of the dwarfs always remained beside it and kept watch over it.

Even the birds of the air came and

mourned for Snow White; first an
owl, then a raven and last of all a
little dove.

Snow White lay a long time in the
coffin and she always looked the same,
just as if she were fast asleep. Her skin
was still as white as snow, her lips
and cheeks as red as blood, and her
hair as black as ebony.

Now it happened one day that
a prince was in the forest and
stopped at the dwarfs' house. He
saw the coffin on the hill with

the beautiful Snow White inside and when he had read the golden letters, he said to the dwarfs: "Let me have the coffin. I'll pay you whatever you like for it."

But the dwarfs said: "Not for all the gold in the world would we part with it."

"Well, then," he replied, "let me have it as a gift, because I can't live without seeing Snow White. I will cherish and love it as my dearest possession."

He spoke so sadly that the good dwarfs had pity on him and gave him the coffin, and the prince made his servants bear it away on their shoulders. Now it happened that they stumbled over a bush and jolted the coffin so violently that the poisoned bit of apple Snow White had swallowed fell out of her throat. Before long she opened her eyes, lifted up the lid of the coffin and sat up alive and well.

"Where am I?" she cried.

The prince answered joyfully, "You are with me," and he told her all that had happened. He also told her he loved her better than anyone in the whole wide world and asked her to go with him to his father's palace and be his wife.

Snow White consented and went

with him, and the marriage was celebrated with great pomp and ceremony.

Now Snow White's wicked step-mother was one of the guests invited to the wedding feast. When she had dressed herself very beautifully for the occasion, she went to the mirror, and said:

"Mirror, mirror on the wall,
    Who is the fairest one of all?"
and the mirror answered:
"You, my Queen, are fair, 'tis true,
    But Snow White is
                fairer far than you."
When the wicked woman heard
these words she was beside herself
with rage and mortification. At first,

she didn't want to go to the wedding at all, but at the same time she felt she would never be happy till she had seen the young queen. As she entered, Snow White recognized her and nearly fainted with fear; but red-hot iron shoes had been prepared for the wicked queen and she was made to put them on and dance till she fell down dead.